# The Peddler
# and the
# Disenchanted Mirror

Rev. Dn. Stephen Muse

# The Peddler and the
# Disenchanted Mirror

*Illustrated by*

Dmitra Psichogiou

Greek-English
bilingual edition, 2016

Edition
PARRISIA

English Edition, 2016

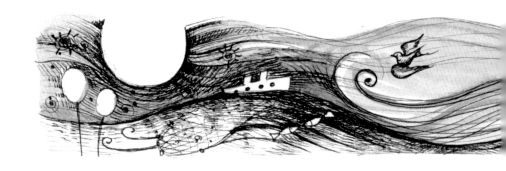

# PREFACE

**T**HERE IS A TALMUDIC SAYING, "We don't see the world as it is but as we are". The Un-created Creator loves to hide from us, clothed in the infinite possibilities of all our faces. Between the mystery of human origins and the deepest yearning of the hidden human heart, there lies an enchanted realm. As in the example of Adam and Eve, we are, each one of us, bedeviled by the illusion that we can find fulfillment entirely in the created realm without ever discovering the true meaning, purpose and intention of being gifted with the potential to become *persons*.

Like the proverbial kiss of the prince upon the lips of Sleeping Beauty, or the beautiful maiden whose love breaks the spell of the beast who becomes a prince, we seek in the faces of those around us, reflections capable of revealing who we truly are.

In my hunger to be, each person's face becomes a mirror in whose gaze I seek the warmth of a reflection that

confirms my existence. But when I look upon the other, the enchanted curse causes me to see an image distorted by my own imperfections, and my need to be rendered perfectly. But what happens when there is no illusion? Is it possible to stand before the other in real relationship without distortion?

*The Peddler and the disenchanted Mirror* is a story of a woman in search of her perfect image. One day at a dusty flea market she finds an unusual mirror, which she tries to purchase to add to her collection. Her struggle with the mirror, the peddler and herself changes her forever.

The story can be read on its own for enjoyment, but buyer beware, it is an enchanted fairy tale. Once read it will not ever entirely be forgotten. You may find yourself in the same position as the woman, with something awakening that will not easily go back to sleep, setting you in search of what she finds. I wish this for all who dare to read it.

*«For now we see in a mirror dimly,*
*but then face to face»*
(I Cor. 13:12)

 PEDDLER spread his wares out on a table in the midst of a dusty flea market.

He had beeswax candlesticks, gold rings of various sizes, a pair of worn leather sandals, some incense and other odds and ends. But most of all he had an assortment of mirrors, some small and some large.

There were mirrors with beautiful ornate frames of bright colors and plain wooden ones worn smooth with age. All of the mirrors had scratches or were warped in some way due to their extreme age. All except for one...

This mirror had a glass so clear and perfect that it seemed to be an empty oval, surrounded by a simple oak wood frame, glowing with the warmth of hand-rubbed beeswax and olive oil.

The peddler was massaging the golden mixture into the frame moving with the grain of the wood when he noticed a woman out of the corner of his eye as she paused to look.

"You have the most unusual assortment of mirrors I have ever seen!" she announced, breathless with desire. The curve of the oak seemed almost responsive to his broad thumbs, flattened from what must have been a lifetime of woodworking.

The woman noticed the quality of feeling his hands expressed as he worked in the paste he poured from an equally ancient alabaster flask beside him. "He must really value the mirror", she concluded.

"What are you polishing the wood with?"

"Olive oil from trees in my father's garden", he replied, without looking at her. "And beeswax from my mother's hives. You can still smell the honey made from the spring blossoms of the apple orchard".

The woman imagined his parents must be very old indeed as the peddler seemed nearly as ancient as the frames scattered around him. His long thick beard had more white hairs than black, including a few stray wood shavings that managed to hitch a ride.

"I can see that you appreciate fine things", she purred. She was experienced in making deals in a very friendly way. She knew from her first glance that she wanted this mirror, but she would be ever so coy.

"The oak tree is sturdy. Its roots extend as deep into the ground as its branches reach up to the sky. It's the favored wood for making wine casks as well as the one most often chosen by the Roman Empire to make crosses".

"What an odd reply", she thought to herself, a little disturbed because the man did not look at her directly and because he was talking about such strange things. Used to being in control, she quickly changed the subject back to her interests. She decided a more direct approach might serve her better.

"I *collect* mirrors," she announced proudly with an air of feigned humility designed to capture his interest. He must surely desire to make a sale. Judging by the tattered old clothes he wore, she was certain that he was badly in need of money.

"What do you do with them?", asked the peddler, now looking at her directly.

She found his eyes were large and unsettling. One seemed kind and gentle; the other alert and perhaps aware of more than she wanted to reveal. She turned away, feigning less interest than she felt and trying not to let her inner response be made known. After all, her purpose was solely to obtain the mirror, not to get involved in some sort of relationship with the peddler.

"I am always in the market for a unique mirror. I have never found the one that I believe accurately reflects me as I am. My search is for the mirror capable of reflecting a truly authentic image". She forced herself to keep eye contact with the man. "If you had one, you could see how to keep your beard free of wood shavings!", she teased.

"I have just the one you are looking for", the peddler smiled, much to her satisfaction, as he fingered a loose wood shaving, removing it from his beard. She felt relieved that she had finally found the way to get his attention on *her* terms. "That's the way to make a deal!" she clucked to herself.

"And which one is that?" she asked obligingly, with a little knowing smile appearing at the corners of her mouth.

"It's one of a kind. Absolutely unique". He wiped his hands on the fragrant rag on the bench beside him and held up the mirror which seemed to her like an empty oval surrounded by a feint glow. The woman looked carefully at it surprised that unlike all the rest, this mirror seemed so clear that it was virtually invisible.

"It's very plain", she said quickly in a disappointed tone designed to distract her adversary so he would lower his price. Even though he hadn't even quoted her a price yet, once she had determined she wanted to possess something, its owner became her opponent regardless of what the asking price was. She was an old hand when it came to negotiating a good deal and the challenge made her feel a pleasant warmth in her body as it consumed all her attention.

"The price for this mirror is as unusual as the mirror", he said matter of factly.

This was going to be more difficult than she realized.

"I'm sure it is. How much are you asking for it?", she inquired dryly, as she continued non chalantly looking at other pieces. She needed a specific number to start with. "Surely it can't be much. It's a small mirror with a simple uncarved frame..."

Interrupting her performance, the peddler responded quietly, "You can have it for nothing or for everything". Had she detected a trace of impatience in his actions? Perhaps he was beginning to smell a sale in the making and was a bit over eager, she thought.

The woman managed a little sarcastic sniff of a laugh at this odd reply. "What kind of price is that?" she needled. "You are just going to *give* it away?"

"If that is your choice", the peddler continued. "As I said, you can have it for nothing or for everything".

"What kind of choice is that!" the woman snorted, a little irritated now by the peculiar turn in the events of her familiar and very skillful way of negotiating with salesmen. "You mean you are not going to charge me *anything* for it?" She'd never encountered such a strange response before.

"The mirror is priceless", the peddler continued. "In fact it is disenchanted."

"You mean enchanted, don't you?", she laughed.

"No, the mirror reveals things exactly as they are without illusion. It illumines whatever motivates the person who looks into it. You could say the person's soul is re-

flected in the mirror, an authentic image if you will. This mirror has a long history and once belonged to King Solomon himself".

The woman laughed out loud at so preposterous a comment coming from this increasingly transparent ploy to get her to raise her offering. He was really overplaying his hand. Opening a little leather purse she picked out a gleaming gold coin and with a slight flourish of her hand, she said as though she were now doing him a favor, "How about this? That should about cover it".

She reached out to hand the coin to him thinking she was indeed getting a marvelous deal for so old and fine an antique with such a perfect reflecting surface. It may not have belonged to King Solomon, but her keen experi-

enced eye for antiques told her it was surely centuries old at the very least. It was indeed remarkable to be in such perfect condition.

"I'm sorry but that is insufficient".

"Adding another from her purse without hesitation", she was still thrilled with the deal, but the peddler was unmoving.

"Oh all right!!", she gasped, appearing to be tired of haggling. "You're more shrewd then I thought", she sniped, as she pulled out a third gleaming coin, insistent within herself that she would now have this mirror for a mere handful of gold. If not satisfied she could easily sell it for double that price.

"The price of the mirror is nothing or everything". The peddler repeated.

"You're telling me that I can have the mirror for nothing at all – that you are willing to *give* it to me but not

for three gold coins? They are worth five times their weight. How much do you want for it?"

"I will give it to you for nothing or for everything. It is your choice".

Bemused and surprised at the strange path the conversation was taking, she found herself laughing with the absurdity of it all and expecting still another surprise if she played along with him. So she announced, "Okay then, I'll have it for nothing".

The peddler carefully covered the mirror with some finely woven cloth and handed it to her gently making sure she had taken hold of it before letting go. "If for any reason you are dissatisfied I ask only that you return it to me".

"Yeah, right, I know, a money back guarantee! I tell you what, if I'm not pleased with it, I'll bring it back to you. At the rate you're going, you wont be making much money and you may need it to sell again to someone less naive than me!"

The peddler smiled warmly and followed her with interest as she turned and walked away.

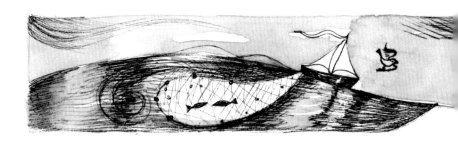

The next day just as the flea market was opening, before many people had arrived, the woman rushed in toward the old peddler who was setting his mirrors out on the table. He looked up at her calmly, noticing the urgency in her gait. It was obvious that she was now on a sort of mission. He felt her eyes locked on him. Her gaze conveyed that unusual and unmistakable expression he had seen before in the eyes of other people who had looked into the mirror and returned to speak with him about what they had seen.

"You tricked me!" she said icily. "This mirror is a fake. It's like the Emperor's clothes. You sold me an empty frame. No wonder it looked so clear. There is no glass in it at all". She was beside herself with a passion that surprised her —one of both defeat and hope and other contradictory overtones— a mixture of feelings she had never felt before.

"How do you know?", the peddler asked calmly.

"Because when I looked into it there was no reflection coming back to me. It's empty", she stormed. She was about to say "I want my money back!", when she caught herself. She blushed at the thought of how embarrassed she would be if she had said such a foolish thing.

"Thank you for bringing it back to me. You are a woman of your word at least. I'm sorry you did not find it useful".

The woman continued to hold the mirror in her hand, wrapped in the same finely woven cloth that the peddler had used when he gave it to her. Something in her would not allow her fingers to let go of it. "How could it be useful when it is not a mirror at all? It's just an empty frame, a beautiful one at that. But you misrepresented the sale!"

"It is a mirror. I told you that. A *disenchanted* mirror".

"Magic! You are full of old tales, peddler. It's a good thing you didn't charge me anything for it or I would report you to the owners of this market as a dishonest merchant!", she fumed.

"I was honest with you madam. I told you the price of the mirror and you made your choice".

"What's that got to do with it? Your foolish riddle – all or nothing? That's nonsense! You claim it is a mirror, but it is simply an old wooden frame. You are a LIAR!" She couldn't believe she'd uttered those words with such vehemence and wondered what kind of response he would make.

The peddler's silence made her a little uneasy and increased her curiosity all the more. He did not seem taken aback in the least by her charade but looked at her with those soulful eyes that made it hard for her to distrust him and hard to be angry. She found herself actually being truthful for a change.

"What if I had chosen differently? What if I gave you six gold pieces for the mirror? Would that make a difference?", she asked, wondering if paying a fair price would change the outcome.

"I'm afraid not. The mirror is priceless".

"Priceless! What does that mean? You won't take anything for it – I mean, you will give it away for nothing and yet you won't take any amount of gold for it. You're not making sense!" She was pleading now, thirsting to fathom something that was beginning to press upon her heart beyond her reasoning mind hungering for understanding.

"Perhaps you would like to change your mind?"

"What do you mean?" she asked, uncomprehending.

"I mean would you like to make a different choice? Everything depends on that. You are free to choose".

"You mean give you all the gold I have?" She wondered where those words came from. The woman was becoming afraid now. Not because she didn't want to give everything for the mirror, but because she was aware that in some uncharted depth of her heart, she *did* want to. And she had accumulated quite a lot of money in her lifetime through very shrewd dealings and an iron will.

"I am not talking simply about money. I mean *everything.*"

"Oh I get it", she said sarcastically, reverting back to her old calculating self. Yet a strange but pleasant, almost familiar fear was beginning to well up within her. It was a lot like... like love. "You mean I can get you to give me the mirror for nothing or for everything I have?" Her lips moved while her heart pondered this strange new feeling.

"Not exactly, you can't *get* me to give it to you. It isn't a *deal* or a trick or a business transaction. It is a pure gift. I am willing to give you the mirror for nothing or for everything. It has always been so. Your choice makes the difference in how the mirror works, but the gift is the same".

"I don't understand", she said, now truly frustrated and wondering why she was spending her morning talking with a strange old man who spoke in riddles, yet not wanting to turn away. "What are you asking of me!" she blurted out now as exasperated with herself as with him.

"I'm not asking anything. You are the one who approached me and asked for the mirror. I'm simply offering it to give it to you as you have requested".

"But it doesn't work!", she shouted, momentarily loosing her composure and quickly regretting it.

"That depends on what you give for it. I am willing to give it to you, but you must be willing to give something in return to receive it".

"Aha! I knew there was a catch!" She was relieved now, but strangely, also a little disappointed. "And what is that?", she continued. "I'm certainly not willing to give you more than it is worth!" She was falling back into her old pattern again.

"I wouldn't expect you to", the peddler replied. "But if you give nothing for it, why would you expect to discover anything in return?"

"Now wait just a minute. I offered to give you six gold pieces for it. That's a fair deal. Frankly, I'd willingly give you a thousand for it if it was really enchanted, but that's beside the point. You told me you'd give it to me for nothing and that was the deal".

"It is not a deal", he reminded, "and it's not magic".

"Okay, okay. I gave you nothing and you gave me a *disenchanted* mirror just as you said you would. I took it home and opened it up and looked into it and there was nothing there".

"I understand."

"Nothing!"

"That's right, nothing plus nothing equals nothing".

"Oh, I get it", she reasoned. Your game is to swindle me out of as much as you can for that silly old mirror and then take off before I have time to find out it's a fake! Let me tell you, you're the best flim flam man I've ever had the pleasure to meet!"

Her hands were shaking now. She needed to believe this. Otherwise only one option remained. It made her uneasy, yet attracted her like a moth to a flame. She could neither understand nor ignore the call she felt deep within

her. She wanted that mirror. It had begun to take on an urgency for her, like life and death. What if the peddler was telling the truth? Suppose the mirror was indeed disenchanted and could render the truly authentic image she had been searching for her whole life...

She was quiet for a moment, suddenly remembering the lines she heard as a girl in a favorite fairy tale, "Mirror, mirror on the wall, who's the fairest of them all?". If the mirror was alive in some way, it would need to be valued...or perhaps she herself would need to be valued. It was confusing...

"Are you all right?", the peddler asked after a few minutes.

Startled, she spoke up quietly as from far away, "Yes... yes I'm fine". She was quiet again for a moment and then said humbly but without hesitation, looking directly into the peddler's eyes. "What if I am willing to give everything for the mirror? Will you take it?"

"No, I will give the mirror to you. Everything and nothing are the same to me".

"What do you mean?" she asked, truly not understanding. "I am now willing to give everything for the mirror".

"I understand", he said, "and I am glad. The mirror is priceless. You cannot give anything to buy it or pay for it. I am willing to give it to you for nothing or for everything. The choice is yours and it makes all the difference in the world. Think very carefully what the mirror is worth to you. If it is truly capable of revealing the authentic likeness that you have been in search of your whole life, then you will know its true value and you will no longer be concerned about its price".

"Okay. Give me the mirror for everything", she said, not fully understanding what she was saying, but having sincerely assented in her heart to find out. For some reason, she no longer considered the peddler her enemy, but a kind of mysterious friend.

The old trader carefully wrapped the mirror in the same finely woven cloth that he had before and handed it gently to the woman whose hands now trembled as she received it. She was on the verge of tears.

"Thank you! Thank you! Thank you!", she said, her heart now more grateful than she had ever felt when she purchased something with her money or her cleverness and charm. It was a feeling entirely different than anything she had ever known in her business dealings.

She suddenly felt gratefully unworthy, as though given a priceless treasure. She found herself weeping as her heart gently expanded to embrace a warm spreading light – a light that revealed every unkind word she had ever spoken, every miserly deal she had ever made, yet filled her with unexpected hope and gladness.

This was a joyful sorrow as paradoxical as the priceless mirror itself; absolutely worthless and yet infinitely beyond value. She had no words to express the growing wonder that was spreading within her.

Without turning back to her home, she unwrapped the mirror on the spot and looked into it, not sure what she might see, and no longer really caring, for she had already

begun to discover an authentic image in the mirror of her own heart.

As she gazed into the oval, her newly found image appeared even more brilliantly. Gazing more intently, from deep within herself, she witnessed an astonishing sight.

The peddler's strange and wonderful eyes now looked back at her through her own. This wondrous effect only deepened the clarity arising in her heart.

Suddenly she felt she could no longer bear to look. The intensity of the peddler's eyes filled her with such love and shame.

Gratefully she fell to her knees. Tears streamed from her eyes as a thousand chains fell away from her and a thousand longings found new hope.

Endlessly flowing streams of love welled up within and overflowed in sighs too deep for words.

Carefully and tenderly she wrapped the mirror back in the finely woven cloth and placed it at the peddler's feet.

"Give this to another. It is too precious for me alone to possess", she said softly. "It must be shared".

She felt the peddler's large warm hands on her head, touching her tenderly as she had first noticed him caressing the frame around the mirror. Only now did her eyes notice the small rectangular scars on each of his feet illumined by a soft golden glow and smelling of beeswax, olive oil, incense and honey.

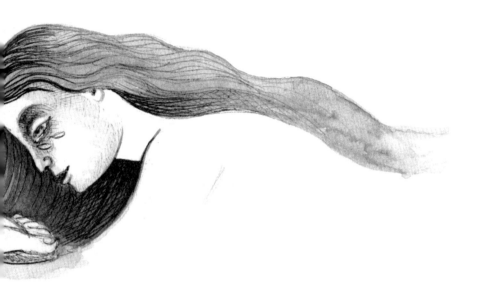

Christ you are the true yearning
and inexpressible joy
of all who love you.

From anonymous prayer after Eucharist

# Bibiliographical sketch

Rev. Dn. Stephen Muse, Ph.D., LMFT, CCMHC, B.C.E.T.S is director of Education and Counselor Training at the Pastoral Institute, Inc. in Columbus Georgia where he directsClergy-in-Kairos, a week-long intensive out-patient stress and wellness program for clergy and their spouses. He has served as a part-time instructor in the graduate counseling program of Columbus State University, as adjunct faculty with the doctoral programs of Garrett Evangelical Seminary in Illinois; Union Graduate Institute in Ohio and the D.Min. programs of Columbia Theological Seminary and McAfee School of Theology in Atlanta, GA. He taught and supervised in the U.S. Army Family Life Chaplain Training program at Fort Benning from 1995-2015 and has served as a clinical field supervisor for Auburn University counseling psychology program. Fr Stephen has taught and led workshops throughout the U.S. and Internationally in the areas of his specialties which include clergy stress and wellness; healing and growth from trauma, moral injury and spiritual pain, training pastoral counselors, marriage as a spiritual path and ascetical psychology.

His books include *Beside Still Waters: Restoring the Souls of Shepherds in the Market Place* (2000); *Raising Lazarus: Integral Healing in Orthodox Christianity*, (2004) and *When Hearts Become Flame: An Eastern Orthodox Approach to the διά-Λογος of Pastoral Counseling.* (2011) (Greek Edition in 2014) and *Being* Bread (2013). He has contributed chapters in numerous books, and is author of some 60 articles and book reviews for various professional and trade magazines including national award winning research in the area of religious integration and clinical empathy of therapists. His work has been translated into Russian, Greek, Swedish and Serbian. He served as Managing Editor of *The Pastoral Forum* from 1993 to 2002.

Fr. Stephen holds a bachelors degree in philosophy from Davidson College, an M.Div. from Princeton Theological Seminary where he studied with Fr. Georges Florovsky. He has M.S. and Ph.D. degrees from Loyola University of Maryland in Pastoral Counseling and completed post graduate work in marriage and family studies through the University of Georgia. He is a Diplomate in the American Association of Pastoral Counselors; Diplomate Board certified in Traumatic Stress and in Professional Psychotherapy and clinical hypnotherapy. He is an AAMFT Approved supervisor, Certified Clinical Mental Health Counselor, and ministry coach.

Prior to his entry into the Greek Orthodox Church in 1993 he pastored a Presbyterian congregation for 11 years and helped begin an out-patient psychiatric clinic in Delta, PA. He serves on the Assembly of Canonical Bishops Pastoral Praxis Committee, is past president of the Orthodox Christian Association of Medicine, Psychology and Religion and is a founding member and first parish council President of Holy Transfiguration Greek Orthodox Church in Columbus, GA where he now serves at as a deacon. He and his wife Claudia have three grown children and three grandchildren. They lost a 6 year old in an accident in 1982.

## About me

I was born and raised in Halkida. Ever since I was a child I loved making things with my own hands and I enjoyed reading fairytales. In 1990 I studied art, design and decoration at Vakalo. It was during a trip to Crete, on a spring day in 1994, that I decided to settle there. I lived in Crete for 13 years, till 2008, teaching art to both young children and adults. At the same time I attended Icon painting lessons under the guidance of Georgos Kordis, whose/an art that deeply influenced me. I entered the enchanting world of fairytales in 2004 and it was then when I realised that each one of us has a special way to express his feelings about the things he loves. My way is fairytales. I have been giving art lessons to young and older children at my workshop 'rock-paper-scissors' (petra-psalidi-harti) since 2009.

*www.nadeenshoes.com • www.petra-psalidi-xarti.gr*

The Peddler
and the Disenchanted Mirror

*Author:*
Stephen Muse

Illustrator:
Dimitra Psichogiou

Bilingual edition: Athens 2016

ISBN: 978-960-696-205-9

**First American Edition**

ISBN-13: 978-1537642819

ISBN-10: 1537642812


Editions Parrisia


2, Ioanninon str.,
183 45 Moschato - Greece
Tel. (+30) 210 94 22 075
e-mail: parrisiabooks@gmail.com
www.facebook.com/parriasiabooksgr

Made in the USA
Columbia, SC
09 July 2017